MAIASAURUS

"Good Mother Lizard." These dinosaurs nested together in bowl-shaped mud mounds. The adults were 30 feet (9 m) long and 15 feet (4.5 m) tall. The babies were 3 feet (1 m) long and 12 inches (30 cm) tall.

MAIA

A young female Maiasaurus. When she hatched, she was 3 feet (1 m) long and 12 inches (30 cm) tall.

DAZZLE

An imaginary dinosaur hatched from an extraordinary egg. The baby Dazzle was 3 feet (1 m) long and 12 inches (30 cm) tall. A fan of reflecting spines ran along his back and down his tail.

STEGOSAURUS

"Plated Lizard." With remarkable plates along its spine, the Stegosaurus was about the size of an elephant, 11 feet (3.4 m) tall and 25 feet (7.5 m) long. The hips were the highest point, and Stegosaurus carried its head low to the ground to help find plants to eat.

DEINONYCHUS

"Terrible Claw." This fast-moving biped was 9 feet (2.7 m) long and 5 feet (1.5 m) tall. It had long hands with sharp claws; the second toe of its foot had a knifelike claw that was 5 inches (13 cm) long. It probably hunted dinosaurs much larger than itself.

For brave girls, shy boys,
and everyone who likes adventure

**OTHER BOOKS
BY MARCUS PFISTER**
◆ ◆ ◆ ◆
**THE RAINBOW FISH
THE CHRISTMAS STAR
PENGUIN PETE
PENGUIN PETE'S NEW FRIENDS
PENGUIN PETE AND PAT
PENGUIN PETE, AHOY!
PENGUIN PETE AND LITTLE TIM
HOPPER
HOPPER HUNTS FOR SPRING
HOPPER'S EASTER SURPRISE
CHRIS & CROC**

Copyright © 1994 by Nord-Süd Verlag AG, Gossau Zürich, Switzerland
First published in Switzerland under the title *Der kleine Dino*
English translation copyright © 1994 by North-South Books Inc.

First published in the United States, Great Britain, Canada,
Australia, and New Zealand in 1994 by North-South Books,
an imprint of Nord-Süd Verlag AG, Gossau Zürich, Switzerland.

Distributed in the United States by North-South Books Inc., New York.

Library of Congress Cataloging-in-Publication Data is available
A CIP catalogue record for this book is available from The British Library.
ISBN 1-55858-337-8 (TRADE BINDING)
ISBN 1-55858-338-6 (LIBRARY BINDING)

3 5 7 9 TB 10 8 6 4 2
3 5 7 9 LB 10 8 6 4 2
Printed in Belgium

DAZZLE
THE DINOSAUR

BY MARCUS PFISTER

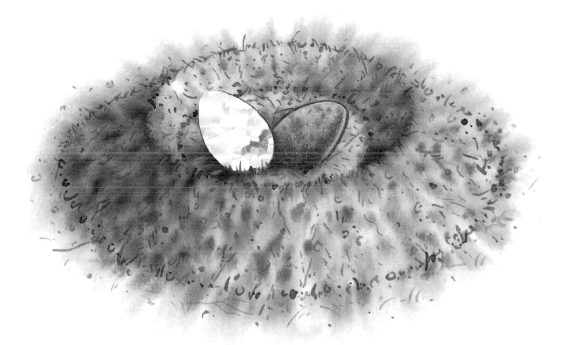

TRANSLATED BY J. ALISON JAMES

NORTH-SOUTH BOOKS
NEW YORK · LONDON

When Mother Maiasaurus came back to her nest, she was surprised to find another egg next to her own. It certainly was not *her* egg.

"Where could it have come from?" she wondered. Instinctively she covered up both eggs to protect them. The valley was a dangerous place. Food was scarce and water was hard to find. There were even some dinosaurs who raided nests as soon as a mother's back was turned.

The other Maiasauruses were curious about this odd-looking egg. As soon as the two eggs started to crack, they all came running to see what would hatch.

From the mother's own speckled egg, out stepped a sweet-looking baby girl. Everyone *oo*hed and *aah*ed.

When the other egg started to crack open, they held their breath—but then they sighed: it was just an ordinary baby dinosaur.

The Maiasauruses were about to turn away when the baby dino gave a little yawn, stretched and—*pfflupt!*—up popped a row of glowing spines along his back. They had never seen anything like it. "What kind of dinosaur are you?" they asked.

"I don't know," the little dinosaur said shyly.

Mother Maiasaurus couldn't take her eyes off the glittering spines. "We'll call you Dazzle," she said softly.

Mother Maiasaurus named the little girl Maia, and soon she and Dazzle were the best of friends. Every day they would go out and play, finding fresh shoots and roots to eat. But they were never allowed to go beyond the edge of the trees. Everywhere they turned, there was a Maiasaurus watching, keeping them safe.

One night Maia and Dazzle were awake when they should have been sleeping.

"What are you thinking about?" Maia asked her friend.

"I wish we could go off on our own, and explore without someone watching us all the time," Dazzle said.

"We can't because it's too dangerous around here," Maia said. "The Deinonychus raids our nests and the Tyrannosaurus Rex chases us away from the water."

"Then why do we live here?" asked Dazzle.

"Mother told me that our family used to live in a cave, in a valley surrounded by mountains that kept us safe. There was a fresh spring in the cave, and the valley was filled with trees and ferns."

"What happened?" Dazzle asked.

"Long ago, when mother was young, a vicious Dragonsaurus took over our cave when all the Maiasauruses were out eating. He was so fierce that they had to move away."

"I won't stand for that!" said Dazzle sleepily. "We'll have to chase him out."

"Yes," yawned Maia. "It's up to you and me."

In the morning, the two little dinosaurs couldn't wait to get started on their adventure. They went through the trees, as they did every day. But this time they scampered off and disappeared among the rocks.

Dazzle was a little scared, but Maia cheered him on. "The mountains are nearby. If we climb up these rocks, we'll be able to see them."

Just then the rocks beneath them rumbled and shook. It was an earthquake!

Maia and Dazzle were tossed to the ground. Then suddenly a giant Stegosaurus stood in front of them. Those weren't rocks they were climbing. It was the Stegosaurus's back!

"Why are you two little dinosaurs so far away from home?" asked the kind Stegosaurus.

"We're just playing a game," Maia said quickly.

"You had better watch out," Stegosaurus said. "You are lucky it was me you climbed on, and not a Tyrannosaurus Rex!"

"She's right," said Dazzle. "We probably should go home now."
So Dazzle and Maia turned back for their grove of trees, where all the Maiasauruses would look out for them and keep them safe.

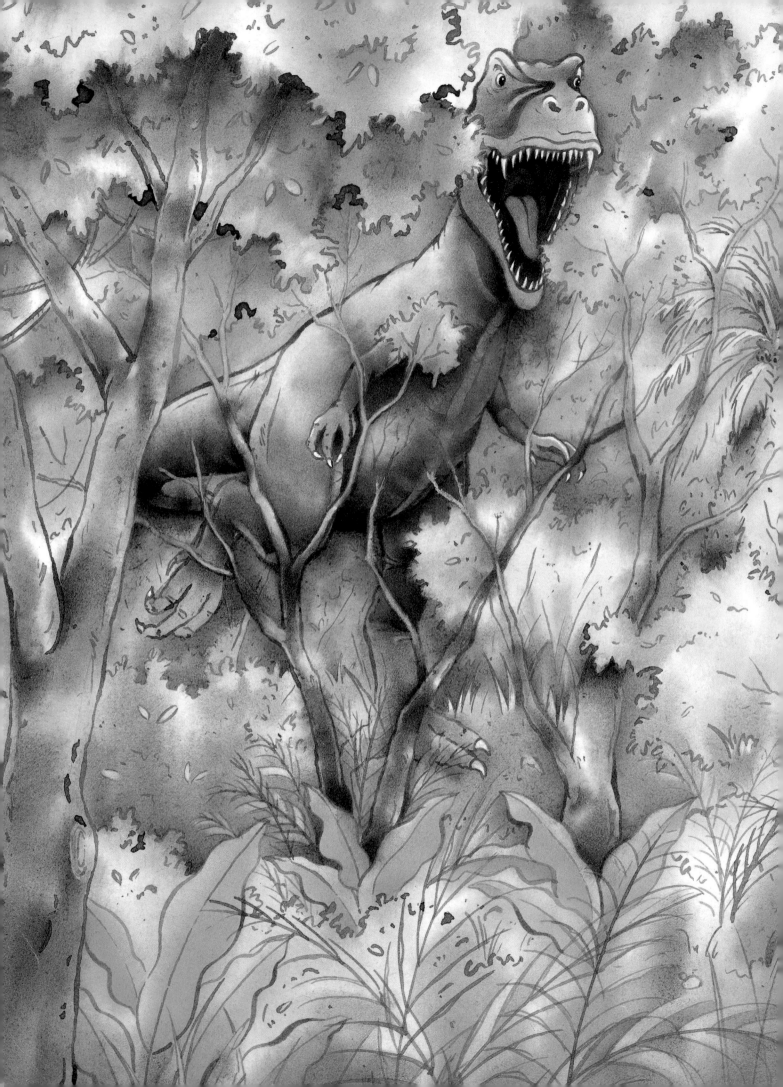

But just as they found some tall ferns to eat, they heard the rumbling thunder of giant footsteps, and an ear-shattering roar. It was a Tyrannosaurus Rex! He had spotted the two little dinosaurs, and he was hungry.

"Split up!" cried Maia. "Twist and turn! Find a place to hide! Run!"

So Dazzle ran away from his friend, dashing under the branches and in and out of shadows. But every time the sunlight flashed on his spines, the Tyrannosaurus Rex gave another roar and came after him.

Finally Dazzle saw a dark grassy hollow, and he curled up inside, keeping his spines from showing. He barely dared to breathe.

Tyrannosaurus Rex lumped and thumped and roared, until finally he gave up. Dazzle waited a long time before he climbed out to find Maia.

"Poor Dazzle," Maia cried as she jumped out of some ferns. "Your spines kept giving you away. You're lucky he didn't catch you!"

Dazzle was just happy to be alive. He wanted a nap.

The two of them found a nice warm tree trunk to lean against, and they fell fast asleep.

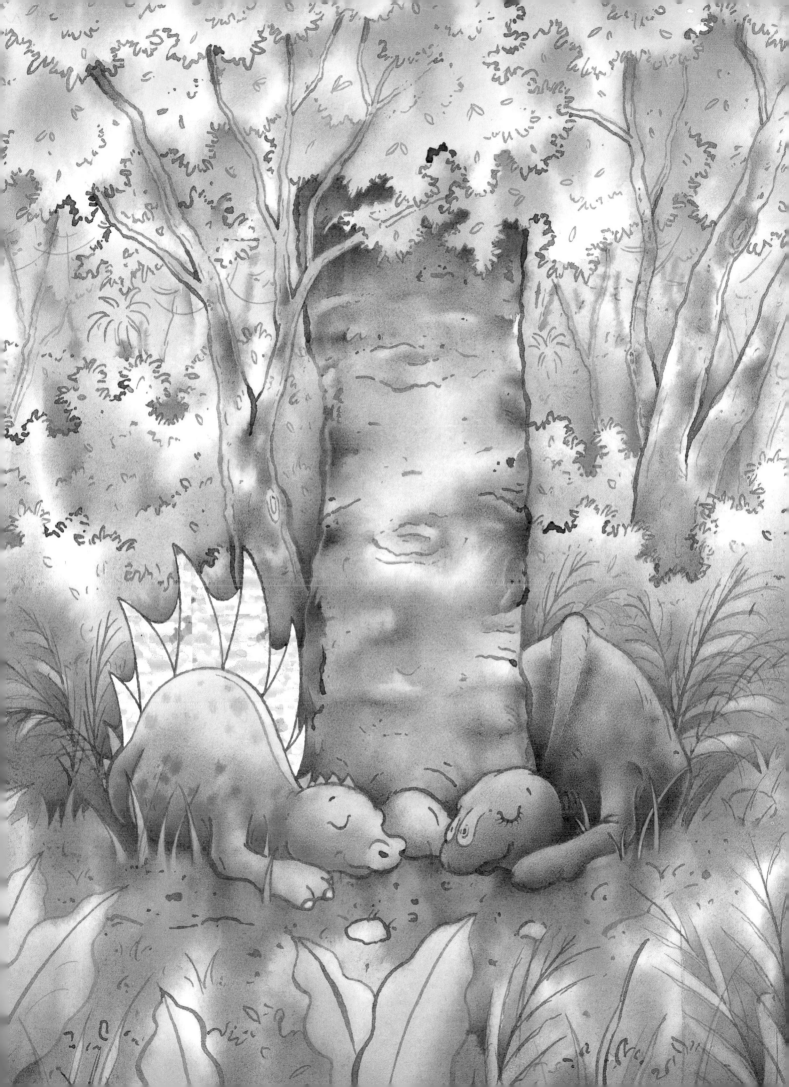

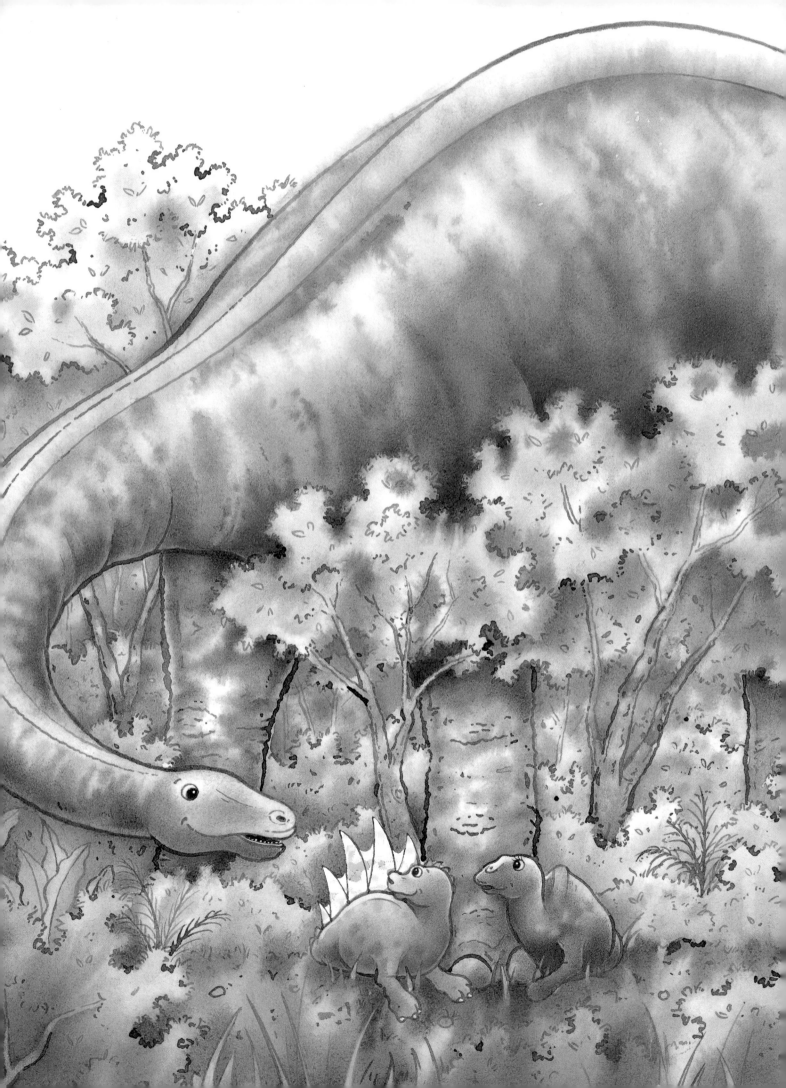

They didn't wake up until their tree trunk lifted up from the ground and shook itself.

"I'm sorry to disturb you," said a deep voice. "But my leg was getting stiff." It was an Apatosaurus. "What are you doing so far from home?" he asked.

Maia decided to tell the truth this time. "We are trying to find the cave where my family used to live."

"But we got lost," said Dazzle. "Could you show us the way—" He wanted to say "home," but Maia interrupted.

"The way to the cave?" she finished.

The Apatosaurus waved his long neck thoughtfully. "The Dragonsaurus is a dangerous dinosaur," he said. "But as long as it is still daytime, I don't see the harm. The Dragonsaurus is terrified of light."

The Apatosaurus reached his head above the trees and called to the flying reptiles for help. Down swooped two Pterodactyls and a Quetzalcoatlus.

"I'll take you there," said the Quetzalcoatlus, who was big enough to carry the two little dinosaurs. "But you have to be ready to go back at sunset. I'm not staying around when that Dragonsaurus wakes up."

They reached the cave just as the afternoon sun shone on the trees in the valley. Nothing had ever looked so beautiful to the little dinosaurs.

They peered into the cave and could see the Dragonsaurus fast asleep. They had to get rid of him so their family could return home. But how?

Maia bravely crept into the cave. Suddenly the Dragonsaurus sniffed, and jumped up, blinking his eyes.

Maia was trapped! The Dragonsaurus gave a mighty roar. Dazzle thought fast. Quickly he turned his back so that every spine caught the sunshine and reflected the light right into the giant dinosaur's eyes.

The Dragonsaurus screamed and ran out of the cave to escape the light, but since it was bright outside as well, the Dragonsaurus just kept running.

Maia and Dazzle took a long drink of water from the fresh spring and went outside to meet the Quetzalcoatlus. "What did you do to the Dragonsaurus?" he asked in amazement. "I saw him running away."

"Dazzle scared him off with his beautiful—*dazzling*—spines!" exclaimed Maia. "He saved my life!"

The Quetzalcoatlus flew the two little dinosaurs back to their family so they could tell everyone the great news. The next day, Dazzle and the Maiasauruses climbed the mountains and settled in their old cave.

"Tomorrow," said Maia, "we can explore our new forest."

"All by ourselves," said Dazzle.

"And you can let your spines shine as much as you want," whispered Mother Maiasaurus. "You'll be safe here."